For Jenn, Julia, and Erin

THIS IS A BORZOI BOOK PUBLISHED BY ALFRED A. KNOPF

Copyright © 2020 by Mark Hoffmann

All rights reserved. Published in the United States by Alfred A. Knopf, an imprint of Random House Children's Books,
a division of Penguin Random House LLC, New York.

Knopf, Borzoi Books, and the colophon are registered trademarks of Penguin Random House LLC.

Visit us on the Web! rhcbooks.com

Educators and librarians, for a variety of teaching tools, visit us at RHTeachersLibrarians.com

The Library of Congress has cataloged the hardcover edition of this work as follows:.
Names: Hoffmann, Mark, author, illustrator.
Title: Dirt cheap / Mark Hoffmann.
Description: First edition. | New York : Alfred A. Knopf, 2020. |
Summary: Birdie wants a very expensive soccer ball but has no money, so she
starts selling dirt and learns some important lessons along the way.
Identifiers: LCCN 2018039755 | ISBN 978-1-5247-1994-4 (hardcover) |
ISBN 978-1-5247-1995-1 (hardcover library binding) | ISBN 978-1-5247-1996-8 (ebook)
Subjects: | CYAC: Moneymaking projects—Fiction. | Soils—Fiction. |
Selling—Fiction. | Humorous stories.
Classification: LCC PZ7.1.H635 Dir 2020 | DDC [E]—dc23

The text of this book is set in 18-point Clarendon LT Std Light.
The illustrations were created using acrylic paint and colored pencil.
Book design by Elizabeth Tardiff

MANUFACTURED IN CHINA
April 2020
10 9 8 7 6 5 4 3 2 1

First Edition

Random House Children's Books supports the
First Amendment and celebrates the right to read.

This is Birdie.

Birdie? Birdie? . . . Say hi.

Hi.

DIRT CHEAP

MARK HOFFMANN

Alfred A. Knopf
New York

What are you looking at, Birdie?

The XR1000 Super Extreme Soccer Ball.

It's so beautiful.
I want it. I <u>need</u> it!

Well, soccer balls cost money.

How much ya got?

Um...none. If only money _did_ actually grow
on trees. Or anywhere for that matter.

Maybe you could sell some of your stuff?

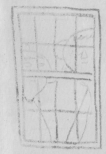

DIRT FOR SALE! DIRT FOR SALE!

High-quality, fresh morning dirt for sale.

That's a hefty price for a bag of dirt. Is that how much you think it's worth?

How should I know what it's worth?

I'm just trying to buy a soccer ball.

You can't expect to make all the money at once. Maybe you should rethink the price.

Psst. Birdie! That is 25 cents! There's actually lots of ways to make 25 cents.

Birdie, you're really onto something here.

Dirt for sale! Come get the freshest, dirtiest dirt anywhere around!

Dirt
Cheap
Cheap
Dirt

1 QUARTER

25 PENNIES

2 DIMES, 1 NICKEL

1 DIME, 15 PENNIES

3 NICKELS, 10 PENNIES

1 DIME, 3 NICKELS

5 PENNIES, 4 NICKELS

And those are just a few of the ways to do it.

How much did you make, Birdie?

Looks like a lot...okay,
let's see...one, two,
three, four, five, six...

You did it! You can buy the
soccer ball of your dreams!

All this is the same as $24.95?

It sure is! You even have a few extra coins to spare.

So this is it, huh? Looks like a great soccer ball.

Right?

Yard?...
Uh-oh!

Oh, hold on! I know what I can do.

Interesting.

Lucky for me, there's plenty of work.